Small Feats & Tall Tales

Charley Elbow

A Book of Poems, Haiku and Very Short Stories

Small Feats & Tall Tales

A Book of Poems, Haiku and Very Short Stories

Small Feats & Tall Tales

Small Feats & Tall Tales

Small Feats & Tall Tales

Small Feats & Tall Tales

Family Foibles and Fables 75

Small Feats & Tall Tales

Small Feats & Tall Tales

Small Feats & Tall Tales

Animal Feats and Tails

Al the Dinosaur

Al the dinosaur
Loved to roam the earth humming
Land, plants and trees shook

Dragons Fly

Dragon hatchlets play
Leaping around in their nest
So eager to fly

Plotting

Veggie patch attacked
Pigeon and bunny chatting
Probably plotting

Cabbage Cat

Chameleon Cat
Camouflaged amongst
Cabbages
Took cruel delight
In making rabbits
Scarper

12 Word Fiction

Unicorn–Frog (Part I)

In a land far, far away
Nobody cares about
The clothes you wear
Whether you're short or tall
A boy or a girl
Or neither
A tree, a pear
Or a bee

A zebra-dog
A unicorn-frog
Or a bumble-giraffe flea
They only care
That you're happy and free

Lucky

Lucky the grey cat
Thought she had ten lives to live
Lucky's luck ran out

Busy Bee

Buzzy, busy bee
Keeps head butting the window
We have no honey!

Blue Bird

Sunlit garden fence
A tiny blue bird peeps through
Playing hide and seek

MisKit Imperious

MisKit imperious and haughty
Rules the neighbourhood
Demanding fidelity, attention
And adoration

Barney the Buffalo

Barney the buffalo
Out in his field one day
Decided to come up with a word
For the green stuff under his feet
That he knew was great to eat

"I think I'll call it poo", he thought
"That's what those things
That wander around looking
Awkward and tall
That I think are called andybobs
Keep shouting out to each other
When they walk around
And put those things they call
Wellybootsandshoes
Down on the ground where I've been"

Small Feats & Tall Tales

You may have noticed that I started this book with some haiku - a form of poem that originated in Japan. All the ones in this book have 5 syllables in the first line, 7 in the second and 5 in the last line. I don't usually like rules in poetry, but I enjoy the challenge of these! I've written some tips on this page in case you'd like to explore writing some yourself.

Nutty Squirrel

There is a squirrel
By the roadside counting nuts
She takes them away
This is descriptive - I wrote what I saw.

I spy a squirrel
By the roadside counting nuts
She takes them back home
This one introduces me as the person seeing it - my participation, and I'm imagining where she is going to go with the nuts.

A brave grey squirrel
So close to the busy road
Happily counts nuts
This introduces emotion - "brave" "happily", and danger - "brave".

Small Feats & Tall Tales

There is no right or wrong with any of the previous ideas, and none are better than any other technically. It's just a matter of taste, and it's fun to play around with them.

Polar Bear

The polar bear cub
Sitting on the bright white ice

...

What last line would you use?

Chuckling Cat

Tim tripped, said naughty words
Parrot repeated them
The Chameleon Cat grinned

12 Word Fiction

Time for Tea

The mole and the vole
Went out for tea
In a glorious hole
Down by the sea

"More tea?" asked the mole
"Yes please" said the vole
In the glorious hole
Down by the sea

"Same time next week!"
Squeaked the vole to the mole
"In our glorious hole
Down by the sea"

MisKit's Band

MisKit's band tempts humans
Into videoing them
So faraway friends
Can watch

12 Word Fiction

Party Animals

Fireflies provided guiding lights
Crickets chirped the music
The octopus conducting
To keep them in time

Herbert the turbot
In charge of the sound
Tipsy the skunk did really well
By not adding to the smell

Belinda the pig in her purple wig
With her natural spots on display
Tiny bugs dancing
Round and around
The decorated horn
Of the unicorn

Party Animals (Cont'd)

Monkeys in onesies
Ants in bikinis
Zebras in top hats and bow ties
Frogs in frocks
Hippos in catsuits
The hedgehogs unsure of the dress code
Wore fabulous open-toed shoes

Dung beetles there just for a feed
Sloths in swimsuits
Otters in tutus
Spiders in ballet pumps
Camels with rainbow ribbons
Adorning their humps

Giraffes in skinny jeans
A sight to behold
Legs stretching up to the sky
The butterflies admired them
As they floated on by

Party Animals (Cont'd)

Everyone was included
With a lake for the fish
The swimmers, the floaters
The water boatmen transporting
Reluctant non-swimmers

The cod and the tuna
Competed together
In synchronised swimming
Axolotls were charming
As were the newts
Snakes politely ate their tea
Well before they arrived

Swifts and swallows
Flew in formation
For a stunning display
Robins and bluebirds
Larks, starlings and puffins
Gaily following behind

Party Animals (Cont'd)

As the dragonflies glinted
In the twinkling lights
The elephant displayed
Her new opaque
Lime green tights

Many wiggled and giggled
Dancing and prancing
To singing and cheers
And vowed to repeat it
Next year

Inquisitive Frog

Inquisitive frog
Left her home for adventure
Lives in our back yard

Decisions, Decisions

Little bird's bum lifts
Deciding whether to launch
Off fence six feet high

Ellie Elephant

Ellie Elephant
Learning to walk the tightrope
Huge mats to catch her

Cat-napping Cat

Chameleon Cat
Lazing on the roof
Gave the squirrel
An almighty shock

Beetle Around

We beetle around with
Bees in our bonnets
Ants in our pants
Bats in our belfries
Flies in our ointments
And soups

We have waspish tongues
Mouths and expressions
Spidery writing
And spidery veins
We're bugged by people
Thoughts and concepts
Germs in our tummies
And eavesdroppers
Whilst being as snug as one in a rug

Unicorn-Frog (Part II)

One bright sunny day
In that land far, far away
The unicorn-frog
And the zebra-dog
Hatched up a plan to have fun
They decided to run
The three-legged race
Imagine the chaos
The scene and the mess
As all of them wished
They had far fewer legs

MisKit's Treats

MisKit deigned to allow
Her chosen humans
To occasionally
Feed her treats

MisKit Plays

After dark MisKit
When sure no-one can see her
Plays like a kitten

Lonely Dragon

The lonely dragon
Made friends with the lively bats
They cling to her wings

Sad Owl

The sad hooting owl
Calls out to the world at night
Is anyone there?

Butterfly Dreams

Butterflies flutter by
Carrying dreams on their wings
Such fragile things, butterfly wings
Carefully carrying our dreams up so high

Hammock

One day in the jungle a hammock
Mysteriously appeared
Strung up between two massive trees

The hamsters, mice and guinea pigs
Shinned up the tree trunks
Scampered along the ropes
And into the hammock
Yippee!
Enjoying some fun in the sun

The squirrels misjudged their angles
Got in a tangle
And just clung on underneath

Chimpanzees and monkeys
Made it look easy
Their young had the temerity
To just launch themselves on top of
Whoever was already there

Hammock (Cont'd)

The sloths looked on
Languidly
Unable to summon the energy
To get involved

Caught Cat

The joke backfired
When Chameleon Cat
Was removed
From Tim's underwear drawer

12 Word Fiction

Labradoodle

Which one would you choose
Labradoodle, cockapoo
Beagle, pug or mutt

Wiggly Worm

Wee wriggling pink worm
Peeking out of damp brown earth
At azure blue sky

Bold Blackbird

Bold little blackbird
Collecting beetles and bugs
To feed hungry chicks

MisKit Reflects

MisKit loves the lake
Gazing at her own image
Reflecting on life

Bearly

Barely awoken
The barely there bare bear spoke
"Don't poke the bare bear!"

Herstories and Histories

Susie Starlight

Susie Starlight
Decided she would
Make an awesome
Private Investigator:
Susie PI

12 Word Fiction

Mystory

I am eccentric
Chaotic sad funny kind
A quiet rebel

Jen's Magic Pen

Jen's red magic pen
Wrote the word poo yet again
She swears innocence

Yourstory

If you sat me down in a corner
With just some paper and a pen
And asked me to write you a poem
I may not be sure where to begin

My ideas seem to be nesting
Deep down in my brain
Only when I'm resting
Do they come out to play

The paper I have around me
Has always been used before
This way it gives me a history
Or maybe even a mystery

Each one of us is different
And has unique tales to tell
I like using poems and rhymes
Haiku are a favourite of mine

Yourstory (Cont'd)

But I know I'm not great
At straight writing
It feels like I'm forcing the words
So I let them tell their own stories
Find their own way out of the pen

There are many approaches
So just take your own time
Find your own rhythm
Maybe your own rhyme

Anya the Brave

"Teachers are bullies!"
Expounded Saffron loudly
To her tribe of acolytes
Who spent their days
Paving her way
To ease her life as their Queen
And their nights in terror
Of her displeasure
For her wrath was immense

Anya the Brave (Cont'd)

She brooked no dissent
She held on to grudges
As if they were trophies
Displayed them to all
Polishing them to a bright
Gleaming shine
As she hinted at deep dark
Revenge

"In what way?" Anya's mouth said
The words escaping
Before she could stop them
She tried not to show
Her surprise
Saffron glared with those
Terrible eyes
And said rather lamely
"Because they make us do things
We don't want to do
By threatening punishment
And flaunting their power over us"
"A bit like you" said Anya's mouth
As it continued its rebellion
Against their monarch

Anya the Brave (Cont'd)

An audible gasp was heard
From her fellow captives of fear
As they looked at each other
Wondering what was occurring
And trying to decide
What to do
Whether to continue to hide
In their own mind
Stand up and be counted
Or just go with wherever
The flow went

'Anya the Brave'
As she was latterly named
In the folklore tales
Of the school
Paved the way
For how others behaved
When faced with
Controllers
Tormentors and terrors
And bullies of their own

Slimy Archie

Covered in slime
And grime
Most of the time
Is little Archie
No one knows why
Or where it all comes from
There's even suspicion
It grows on her skin
But it couldn't really
Surely?

Susie Sultana

Susie Starlight, PI,
Tracks sultanas back
To the suspect's
Open messy cage

Ed's Bed Head

I'm ill you see
I don't have the energy
To spend time with my friends
And I'm scared that
They'll all forget me

I'm confined to my bed
With only the thoughts in my head
To keep me company
So I make up some rhymes
To help pass the time

Now my friends are imaginary-
Superheroes, wizards and ghosts
But the ones I miss most
Are the real friends I had
Missing them is making me sad

Axl's Kite

Little Axl at 5 years old
Deciding to be really quite bold
Planted his feet in the sand.

With long strings in his hands
He prepared for battle
Against the mighty, fierce wind.

His stepdad Jack launched
The beautiful bright kite
And it flew with magnificent ease.

It swooped and it soared
And he knew it could roar
As it cut through the gusts
And the billows above.

Susie Tortoise

Susie, flushed with sultana success
Nearly catastrophically misdiagnoses
Jonathon tortoise's annual hibernation

Ercan and Mo

Ercan and Mo
In their huge battered van
Travelling the world
For adventures
They rarely make plans
Just go wherever they can
Chasing tornadoes, storms
And unicorns

Cushion Cat

Tim, mystified
Searches for his cosy
New cushion
Chameleon Cat wanders away

Susie and the Beans

Susie felt she'd be able to discover
How many beans make five

Different

I do my very best
But I'm different from the rest
I don't look like anyone I know
My Mum calls me her Hero
I'm not really sure what that means

I'm sure I stand out from the crowd
Not in a good way
I try to blend in
And not really be seen
But I'm not too sure that it's working

I know my mum loves me
She tells me so all the time
I'd just like to find my own space in the world
A me-shaped one that is totally mine

Ezri and Me

Ezri and me are a team
I do stuff for him
And he does stuff for me
That's the way it's always been

He can't really read people
Or the wider world around him
Though at maths and physics
He is a real whizz
Even hypothetically at psychology
But he really can't apply it

He looks to me to help him
When he can't read expressions
Or hear voice inflections
He just can't spot them at all
He navigates me around
Computers and books
I help him negotiate life

Ezri and me we're a team

Kami

My hamster Kami
Climbs, jumps, hangs, runs, leaps, plays, hides
Clever and busy

Float Free

On land she is bound
In the air sky sea and dreams
She floats glides swims free

Dancing in my Dreams

Dancing in my dreams
Taking charge of the dance floor
Legendary moves

Susie Socks

Susie, pondering why
All her socks are odd
Interrogates the washing machine

Shoh's Nose

Shoh knows she has a perfect nose
Not too big, not too small
Not too anything at all
How does Shoh know
She has the perfect nose?
'Cos everyone tells her so

Laney's Complaint

Laney said she could have wept
Her hands got all clammy
And covered with sweat
She went to her friend
Barney's house for tea
"I can't believe
What they presented to me"

"A soft boiled egg," she whined
As if this were a heinous crime
"I got all in a flap
And a bit of a dither
And couldn't seem to work out
Whether: To smash in the top
Or cut off its head
So I looked at what other people
Did instead

I can't understand
How they could be so mean
Why couldn't they just give me
Something simple to eat
Like some scones and strawberry jam?"

Small Feats & Tall Tales

Susie Sleep

Susie, investigating mysterious
Nocturnal occurrences
Happily chats to her sleep-walking
Big brother

Tam and Kim

Tam dislikes conflict
His tummy lurches, heart sinks
And palms get sweaty

Kim adores conflict
It sharpens his brain and tongue
Adrenalin rush

Mum is peacemaker
She debates with Kim, hugs Tam
Loves them equally

Puppy Love

I have a beautiful puppy
Booboo is her name
She's little and sweet
Gorgeous and neat
And she adores playing games

She's always with me
Wherever I go, whatever I do
She faithfully keeps me company
And sticks to my side like glue

She listens to all of my troubles
And licks away all of my tears
I tell her all my secrets
And, of course, all of my fears

No one I know can see her
Where I live pets aren't allowed
In my mind she sleeps by the side of my bed
But in reality I know she's just in my head

Find Me

You think you won't like me
'Cos of the way that I look
Take some time
Take another look
It could be worth it
I swear
To find me under there

Susie and the Cat

Susie, PI, recognising the footprints
In the snow
Arrested Chameleon Cat Burglar

12 Word Fiction

Magic, Monsters and Mayhem

Dragon Burps

Dragon burps
Could be a problem for me
You see
I live in a tree house
Made out of wood

Inesa is so friendly
She'd never mean to hurt me
But she is *incredibly* big
Whatever she eats
Gives her hiccups and burps
Then out come swirly flames

And I'll mention again
I live in a house
Made of twigs

But she does always say "Pardon me"

Crooked Stairs

Climbing creepy crooked
Candlelit stairs
Kiren suddenly realized
They weren't really there

Hungry Dragon

The dragon hovers
Hungrily waiting watching
His tummy rumbling

Witches

Witches and wizards
Having a magical time
Everyone spellbound

Drifting

There seems to be something
Deep in my head
Drifting around on my dreams

It may be a bee,
A plane or a flea
Doing the backstroke
In the sea

It could be a canoe
Kayak or yacht
A pirate ship in full sail

A pedal boat, paddle steamer
Or floating igloo
A hummingbird, dragon
Or mosquito

Drifting (Cont'd)

It explores
When I'm sleeping
Taking its powers
From my night-time scheming
Triumphs and mishaps
Happiness or sadness
And anything in between

It gets bigger or smaller
Shorter or taller
As it reacts to the colours
It finds

It's a wonderful thing
As it makes my mind sing
When later I am awake

Magic Boots

Idris knew he was taking a risk
When he borrowed his brother's
Basketball boots

But he needed to find out
If what he thought was true-
Whether they really were magic

If Tom saw they were gone
And told their mum
He'd be in so much trouble

While he was lacing them up
He could feel all his nerves
Turning to steel
Ready to face anything
The game threw at him

He soared and he flew
The court felt tiny
As he took it all in his stride

Magic Boots (Cont'd)

He knew deep inside
That this was it
His one perfect game
And he would never ever
Play basketball again

Katya and the Frog

Katya declined to
Kiss the frog
Unsure that she wants a prince

Purple

His chosen colour is purple
But he's been feeling blue
So he went inside his head
To add in some red

Our House

Our witches live in the kitchen
The bats inhabit the belfry
The attic's got the most ghosts in
The garden's the space the faeries grace
The study is where the gnomes make their home
The roof is where the wise owls are
Of course, our wardrobes lead to Narnia

Hansel and Gretel Reworked

Low carb, gluten free
Hansel and Gretel's
Trail was better
Than breadcrumbs

12 Word Fiction

Haunted Mansion

Huge brass door knocker
On the haunted mansion's door
Have you the courage?

Time Travel

To travel in time
Would be the stuff of my dreams
When would you go to?

MAGIC

Moonbeams
And unicorns' dreams
Gentle beats of hummingbird wings
Imagine mixing all of these things
Creating incredible magic

Animal Magic

I do believe
I'd love to see
A sausage dog fly
Sprout wings and launch
High into the sky
A donkey sing soprano
A basketball-playing rhino
Giraffes pirouetting
Hippos synchronised swimming
Fleas drumming
Spiders strumming
Scuba-diving mosquitoes
Exploring the sea
But the simplest thing
I'd love to see
Is I'd love to see
A cat curtsy

Margaret

There's an old lady
Who lives down our road
You're the first person
I've ever told
I think she might be a witch

She knows when things will happen
And she knows when they will not
She doesn't have a cat
Which, I admit, is odd
But she does walk often
With a big hairy dog
No broom, but a walking stick
That tap tap taps along

I ask her lots of questions
Which she never gets wrong
She talks of shadow dancers
Starstuff, twilight and dawn
Always stands in exactly the same spot
When the silvery moon appears

Margaret (Cont'd)

I see her at midnight gazing at the stars
It seems like she's wondering
Where all her friends are
She's funny and friendly
Witty, warm and wise
When I grow older
I intend being just like her

Slime Monster

The slime monster doesn't
Live under your bed
There is no need
It lives in your head
Not hiding in shadows
But far up your nose
Not in the back of the wardrobe
But deep in your throat
When you get a cold
Or maybe the 'flu
It wakes up the monster
That produces the goo

Safra Stripe (Part I)

Safra Stripe and Henry Hoop
Got married and had
Very cross children

12 Word Fiction

Thunderous Roars

Hot angry summertime rain
Lashing down from the stars
Rattling rooftops and
Flooding the drains
The weather gods are
Happily playing a game
But one of them's cheated
Again and again
So one starts shouting
In thunderous roars
Another replies with
Blisteringly hot words
White lightning flashes
From her furious tongue

Unicorns

Those wonderful horses with horns
Are truly magical beings
I've heard they poo rainbows
And blow fairy clouds out of their noses
What do you suppose you would do
If one visited you for a day?
Maybe go to a land far away
Full of mystery and adventures
Or stay in your room and bathe
In the gentle magic all day
You could go to the mythical land
Under the sea
See creatures you never
Dreamed you could meet
Or laze under the fairy clouds
With rainbows alongside
Or invite all your friends along for the ride
And call up a genie and make the wish
That this day would never
ever
come
to
an end

Mischievous Ghosts

Mischievous old ghosts
Gather for a night of fun
Spooky tricks and treats

Faraway Lands

In faraway lands
Do dragons and unicorns
Often play Quidditch

Spotted Dragon

Seeing the dragon
Hovering watching waiting
Fear prickles my skin

Lewis

I knew Lewis
When we were both
New at this
He knew I could
See straight through him
And he could peer
Straight through me

Now we are
More polished
And definitely
Appear more solid
Than when we were
Whispers of wispy mist

Windmill on the Hill

The crooked windmill
On the crooked hill
Looking oh so quiet and still
Has millions of secrets inside

Hiding in dusty corners
And spaces under the stairs
Are mystical creatures
Weaving magical spells
To surprise and delight
And maybe just frighten a little

Safra Stripe (Part II)

Safra Stripe was starting
To feel invisible
Henry Hoop
Changed their wallpaper

12 Word Fiction

Under My Hat

I have a big secret
I'm trusting you to keep it
I can hardly believe it myself
I have ears just like an elf!
I hide them with hats and my hair
So no one will see them and stare
Or worse, work out what I may be

I'm waiting and watching very carefully
To see if something else may happen to me
Maybe mythical strength or magical powers?
Or the ability to make days out of hours?
It will be brilliant, I'm sure about that
Until then I'm keeping it all under my hat

Tortoise and Hare Reworked

One lovely sunny summer's day
Tortoise and Hare
Decide to picnic instead

Chameleon Cat Ghosts

Ghosts playing with
Chameleon Cat
Love it when
He makes them
JUMP

Sailing Ship

Lying on the deck of a sailing ship
In the deep velvet part of night
Watching the stars
And the moon pass by
A truly wondrous sight

Falling asleep and dreaming deep
Of pirates, treasure, adventure
Waking up, surprised to find
Dreams are not always as they seem
Some may be real life

Little Red Reworked

Little Red Riding Hood
Trained as a vet
Specialising in wolf behaviour

12 Word Fiction

Fart Monster

The fart monster
Doesn't hide
Under my bed
It lies in the bed
Above me
It emits noxious smells
And tries not to tell
And hopes the evidence
Won't reach my nose
As if he doesn't know
This will happen

The fart monster
Emits the gas
As he wanders
From room to room
In the gloom
And thinks that the pong
Won't follow him along
As he tries
To flee the scene

Ghost Shadows

Ghosts in the shadows
Playing games of hide and seek
Not one can be found

Miss Muffet Reworked

Little Miss Muffet
Having a bad day
Yelling
Scared a lion away

Humpty Dumpty Reworked

Humpty Dumpty
Trained in Health and Safety
Still fell off the wall

Elves

Some people have an elf
That lives on a shelf
I have one on each shoulder

One is quiet, gentle and sweet
The other is much, much bolder

One encourages me
To follow my dreams
The other's naughty,
Haughty and screams

But one thing they both say
Above anything else is
Never forget you are loved

Cocooned

Memories and fears
Fly in midnight skies
Some becoming
Cocooned by dreams
Emerging as changelings
Of ethereal matter
Where reality and imagination
Have some tea and chatter
In comes the Cheshire Cat
And a scary Mad Hatter
Nothing is quite as it seems
The March Hare, a Turtle
And the Dreams Keeper
All turning the sleeper
The dreamer, into a…

"Wake up, you're having a nightmare!"

Family Foibles and Fables

Blister Sister

My little sister
Is a really big blister
Under my skin
I want to go out
She wants to stay in
She screams and she shouts
Always running about
Demanding attention
Causing so much tension
Between my mum and me

Brother Below

It's not fair
That I have to share
A bedroom with my brother

He's older than me
Which frequently
He reminds me of

He's the one in charge
He has the top bunk
So I sleep below

As he tosses and turns
As he dreams as he sleeps
The bed springs creak
And keep me awake

So I'm grumpy and cranky
Which makes mum a bit angry
She wonders why I'm exhausted
And acts like it's all my fault.

Grotty

Dad feels so grotty
All snotty and green bogies
Must have a bad cold

Dad's Diet

Dad's on a diet
No sweets bread cakes beer pasta
He's rather grumpy

Pops

There was a loud sneeze
Then a great big wheezy cough
Pop's sweeping chimney

Cousin Greg's Awesome Head

My cousin Greg
Has a really big head
And I don't mean
Figuratively speaking
He keeps lots of facts
In that head of his
When I learn new stuff
I can almost feel
The old stuff leaking
Out of my ears
But nothing escapes
His giant mind
He must have
An awesome filing system
To be able to find
All that detailed information
I always seem to misplace mine
I wonder if he'd let me
Rent some of the space
In his amazing mind?

Nan

I love going to Nan's house
It's always the same
Same smell, same feel
Everything like it's always been
Everything like
It's been arranged just for me

Nan even remembers my
Favourites for tea
I think if I stayed there
For one whole week
She'd cook the bestest things
Every day

My friend Kiran doesn't have a Nan
So I let him share mine
From time to time

Nan (Cont'd)

She asks him questions
Lets him tell her his dreams
And never once laughs
Like his own family does
They just don't see him
As we do

We know he'll be brilliant
He's got so much to say
And he does it all
In his own unique way

My Nan's place is safe
And sort of magic some times
Like it takes care of you
Believes what's in your mind

I wish everyone could have a
Nan like mine
Maybe I could lend her out more
I really don't think that she'd mind

Grandad's Hat

Grandad says he keeps his hat on firmly
To keep his memory in
He says if he were ever to take it off
His memory might fly away

Jak's Grand-Nan

When Jak shows Grand-Nan
What some technology can do
She always asks this of him:
"Who thought up such things?
It's like me dreaming I could fly
Right up to the moon
Using my own arms as wings"

Whiffy Socks

What's that awful smell?
Pizza, bottom burps and socks
My brother's come home

Cheer

Dad gave up the beer
In May last year
'Cos of some good advice

Today he got up off the chair
Gave a really big cheer
"At last I can see my feet"

Quiet Mum

Mum's quiet except
When she sings karaoke
Then she laughs a lot

Queen

My big sister is brill
She's got all kinds of skills
She can sing and dance
Obviously,
She does karate
And thinks herself mighty
She's the diplomat
Sorting things out
For my little sister Mattie
My brother Henry
And me

We call her Dora
'Cos she wants to be
An explorer
Maybe of mountains
Space, or the sea
She can build things
And break things
Into really small pieces
To fit them together again
She can swim and hike and
Grow things in dirt

Queen (Cont'd)

She's funny and cheeky
Can sing under her breath
She keeps adults
Under her spell
She charms little kids
Pretends she's a witch
She wants to end poverty
And hunger and stuff
My Gran says, give her time
She'll be Queen of the Universe
Some day

Snow Cat

When it really thickly snows
I wear my hat with the toasty ear flaps
Jack makes a snow cat
Mo and Bo throw snowballs
I'm the one who slips slides and falls
So to avoid being a danger
I just lie down and make angels

Uncle Toby

My uncle Toby
Once told me
That he used to eat his own bogies
I knew he was joking
When he told me
They tasted like lemon curd

My brother who's younger
Must have overheard
And thought it was true
'Cos he eats his boogers
Morning noon and night

He probes his finger delightedly
All the way up his nose
Tastes it and smiles
Like he's just won the lottery
He gave up on earwax
As he didn't like the smell
And kept trying to put it all back

Yanni's Gran

In one particular moment
My Gran knows who I am
And is funny and clever
And tells us how we are
The best things in her world

Two moments later
She's confused
Calls me by my dad's name
And doesn't know
Why we came

My dad said Gran's brain
Is sort of time-travelling
She can't control it
And can't always remember
Who we are or where she is
Whether she's younger or older

So we just sort of go with it
And patiently wait
Till she comes back to us
In the now

Race

My brother and I
Were having a race
Down the hall in our home
He never stuffs his face
With his chocolate
The way that I do
He carries some with him
For later

He was running at full pelt
When he felt himself falling
Reaching out his hand
To soften his landing
He smeared melted chocolate
All down the wall
It was really funny
But dad didn't think so
At all

The Scent of Sorrow

My Gran calls me her gorgeous boy
She says she's losing her mind
But I think she finds it some days
'Cos she once said to dad
That I had a scent of sorrow around me

You know when you stand near a bonfire
And the smell just lingers on clothes
That's what I think my Gran means

I thought only I could smell it
When I think about dad
But I see that some adults can too
'Cos their faces change when they see me
They don't know how to treat me at all

Dad's really in pain
I'd love us to borrow
Someone else's life for a while
Then we'd be able to see each other
Smile

The Scent of Sorrow (Cont'd)

Some of my mates are great
They don't mind
When I can't spend time with them
As I have to get home
Others don't get it at all

I'd love to hit reset
And start life from the beginning
No, forget that
It's much simpler than that
I just wish I could make my dad better

Light

My brother Stefan
Knows I'm afraid of the dark
He gave me his torch

Auntie Lucie

My mum's smile
Just stays on her lips
Never reaching her eyes
She looks so distracted
Like she's always
Composing some lists
In her mind

But Auntie Lucie's
Coming round today
She's got a smile
That lights up
The whole of our house
It banishes the gloom
To a far away room
That we can play
Hide and seek in

Above and Below the Horizon

The Octopus and the Grouper

I am the octopus
Ed is the grouper
We're a bit of a team
Under the sea
He shows me
The way
To the prey
I poke the space
To scare the prey out
Sometimes he's fed
Sometimes it's me

Ed's not that friendly
But he gives a curt wave
I think he thinks
It'd be a real hoot
If I use all of my legs
In a return salute

Hitching a Ride on a Cloud

Lying on the ground
Looking up at the sky
Watching the clouds
Lazily drifting by
I found myself imagining
What it could be like
To hitch a ride on a cloud

Seeing the world
From way up high
Floating past seas
Lands and lakes
Islands and mountains
Rivers and streams
Forests and plains
Deserts and lush green
Landscapes

Picturing all the people
Inhabiting these places
The animals and creatures
In all of the spaces
I would see

Hitching a Ride on a Cloud (Cont'd)

And all those hidden
From my sight
I may even meet fellow travellers
Up on the cloud
One of those clouds
Drifting lazily by

Bursting Moon

Owls hoot plaintively
Wolves howl and the tides are high
The bursting moon smiles

The Fisher Folk

The sea recalls tales
Of fisher folk and mermaids
In the ocean deep

Variable Stars

Variable stars
Change their luminosity
Rebels of the sky

Dear Weather

Dear Weather

I know I live in the UK
Where skies are often
Cloudy and grey
But since we got
Our telescope
You don't seem to
Have been very kind

Would you mind
Reconsidering
And clear the sky
So the stars
Can come out to play
Please

Exotic Creatures

Underneath the deep blue sea,
Exotic creatures dream of life on land

Underwater Support

Welcome to our support group
Under the sea
Please come in
Where shall we begin?

We have a clown fish that frowns
A pacifist Siamese fighting fish
A neon that can't find its shine
A clam that talks all the time

Our motto is
We are not all the same
And cannot be defined
Just by a name

Underwater Support (Cont'd)

Oh I see,
You say you were
Just floating by
A little bit lost and alone
It happens to most of us
Some days
I'm sure we can help you
Find your way home
Unless you'd like to reconsider
And stay?

Sit on the Moon

I like to go and sit on the moon
To hear the song she sings
I can hear it on quiet, still nights at home
The louder the song
The more peace it brings

Plastic

We used to think that
Plastic was fantastic
In our race to embrace it
We made way too much
Without thinking about
How to safely dispose of it

With no space in
Seabird's stomachs
Because they've ingested
So much of it
We're starving our wildlife
Or wrapping them up in it

What can we do about it?
I guess we could think of:
Ways to reuse it
To stop abusing the planet
Think of alternatives
And give our nature a chance

Muddled

Snowflakes on roses
The seasons are all muddled
The clouds are confused

Stormy Nights

I love looking out
On stormy nights
At firework displays
Of blinding brilliance
With flashes and forks
And sheets of white
Each and every one
Doing their best
To out-shine the rest
Nature reminding us
With her thunderous sounds
That she is the one with the power

Pluto

Poor little Pluto
From Disney dog to planet
Harshly demoted

Saturn

Your glittering rings
Of dazzling icy fragments
Encompass your world

Mars

Planet of red dust
Science fiction inspirer
Home of the rovers

Venus

Monarchs of the night
Mighty moon and Queen Venus
Rule all they survey

Jupiter

Stormy Jupiter
Protector of our planet
What lies deep within?

Entrancing Moon

Headline:
Moon's beauty secrets revealed!
It's her scars that make her entrancing

Spaceship

Through a half-open window
On a starlit night
Gazing at a glorious sky
I spied a puzzling sight

It may have been an optical illusion
Causing me some kind of confusion
Or some refraction of the light

My mind then decided
It was an invisible spaceship
Warping the stars behind it

Could it be from outer space
Full of aliens
Coming to see us?

Icy Tiger

Icy Tiger Enceladus
Saturn's enigmatic moon
What wonders can we learn
From you?
We can hardly believe
What's in front of us
The stripes and the jets
The surprising plumes
All these sights
What will be next?
Is there life below
Your icy surface?
Simple single-celled
Worms or spirals
Or triangle shaped
Axolotls and elves
Goblins and panthers
Dragons that fart methane
Unicorns with rainbow manes
Cyclops and rhinos
Whales and eagles
Spaniels and beagles
Or just squiggly transparent goo?

Lifelines

Beyond Senses

Beyond the range of our senses
Could be exotic objects
Right under our noses

Food we can't eat
Scents we can't smell
More colours we can't see
Could be there as well

In years gone by
Beyond visible light
Infrared and ultraviolet
Hadn't been known of at all

All Cared Out

I'm all cared out today
Usually I care about
Everything and everyone
Anyone I hear of
Everyone I meet
People on TV and the news

Usually I care about
Cats and dogs and mice and frogs
And orang-utans in the forests
And woods
I would never have thought
That I wouldn't care at all
But today I am all cared out

Balloon

The balloon of
Embarrassment
Over his head
Exploded so loudly
It left us all
A bit red

Bubbles

Bubbles appearing from
The washing up liquid bottle
Translucent prisms
Of iridescent beauty

Funny little windy bubbles
Like prisoners mounting
A jailbreak
From your tummy

Bubbles (Cont'd)

Bubbles of nervousness
Taking you by surprise
Bubbles of lies
That expand and expand
Until they explode
Bringing your whole life
Down to its knees

Pleasing bubbles of anticipation
Unexpected bubbles
Of feelings of love
Nasty bubbles of fear and terror
Way down in your stomach
Or far up in your throat

Or lots filling up space in your brain
When you are truly flummoxed
Bubbles of joy laughter and delight
Bubbling streams rivers and dreams
Bubbles to hide in from the rest of the world
Bubbles that protect from pain and sorrow
Bubbles of hope for a brand new bright
tomorrow

Clvr Brains

Have you heard that
Our brains are so clver
That if some vwels
Are remved from some words
They knw them so wll
That they can oftn tell
What the full wrds really are

Random Solutions

Life is so complicated
Each time I try to contemplate it
I reach a different conclusion
Like a computer programme
Written to provide unique
Random
Solutions

Colour and Sound

If today was a colour or sound to you
What colour or sound would it be?
Mine might be the pre-hail grey of the sky
Full of icy shards of all I want to shout
Which could soon come clattering down
Or the calm cool contemplative grey
At the still of dusk
Thinking of things I might like to say
And taking them into the night

The vibrant red of a sports car
Confidently navigating the road ahead
Or the opposite red, the one full of dread
That has us lying in bed
With a cloth on our heads
Waiting for the storm to pass

Colour and Sound (Cont'd)

Or the peaceful calming sound of the bumblebee
Humming its way through life
Without any strife or worries to think of
The cheery yellow of the sunflower meadow
Full of warmth and kindness and light

The roaring sounds of the surf on the rocks
That inspire and cleanse and renew
The fabulous beat of your favourite song
That has you dancing around in your head
With dreams of fame and fortune
Or the lilting tune of your own unique rhythm
That only you know, that guides you through
And keeps your inner light bright

Haiku

Brief yet eloquent
So many stories are told
In five, seven, five

Haphazard

A bit haphazard
All higgledy piggledy
Home brimming with love

Sunny Side

They choose to walk on
The sunny side of the street
Metaphor for life

Eyes

I think you can tell a lot
About most people
If you just look into their eyes

Some, like my grandma's,
Look really wise
Others look like they wish
They were far, far away

Milo's look like he's searching
Somewhere for tomorrow
Nanny's are hard to look into
They are so full of sorrow

I'm really good
At a Paddington hard stare
When I need to be left alone

Pop seems like he's having
Fun in his mind

Eyes (Cont'd)

Jamie squints like she's lost something
She may never find

My favourites are the ones that
Just look loving and kind.

Hurdles

See the hurdles
Lined up in a row
Ready for the race?
Instead of trying
To fight them
Before they reach me
And hoping they might
Not be so high
I'm learning
To face them
Just one at a time
Leaving some space
And
Breathing between

Life

Mum acts like the way
She should live her life
Is carved in a stone
That she reads
And dusts off every day

Dad sees life
As a sort of hallway
With loads of doors
Which if you go thro'
Lead to some corridors
With even more doors

You may lose yourself
A little bit some days
But it's up to you
To choose your own way

There is no map-
Moving forward or back
Or right or left
Is completely at
Your own behest

I Love a Hat

I love a hat
But in the town
Where I am from
If anyone went into
The posh supermarket
Wearing a baseball cap
They'd look with suspicion
Like they thought you'd run off
With a chicken
Or something significantly worse

My Friend

I really miss my friend Penny
So I popped up to the sky
We whirled and we twirled
As we danced way up high
She bowed and I curtsied
As we said our goodbyes

Muzzy Thoughts

My thoughts are all muzzy
And fuzzy today
Trudging around and around
In my head
At different
Speeds
In different
di
r
e
c
ti
ons
I think I grasp one
Then lose the thread
Nothing to hold onto

Some are stomping a bit
In heavy boots
Some clicking and clacking
In heels with sharp points
I'm sure I can hear some
In tap shoes

Muzzy Thoughts (Cont'd)

Tap tap dancing
Around the edges
Some make muffled sounds
In deep cosy slippers
And some have their feet up
And will not walk today.

Navigating Life

Vic floats along the river of his life
Embracing all twists and turns
Never knowing where he'll end up
Excited by what he might learn

Ash thrashes about in the torrents
Of the life he has been given
Dad and Mindy pulling him this way
Mum and Dan pushing him that

Sacha feels he's a traffic cop
Or a captain on the high seas
He navigates the life of those around
Without him they would all drown

Haiku Diary

One thing I especially like about haiku is the way we can fit so much into those 17 syllables. I had the idea of writing a haiku diary for fun, so here it is. Maybe you'd like to try writing one about your day, or starting a diary?

Just had a nightmare
No ghosts or monsters, worse, it
All felt very real

Even on TV
Looking at the sea soothes me
It pleases my soul

Clouds moving so fast
As I walk along watching
They make me dizzy

Haiku Diary (Cont'd)

Granny and Grandad
Shout at each other a lot
'Cos they are both deaf

 Mum's birthday today
I gave her jigsaw puzzles
We ate lovely cake

I am overwhelmed
I feel lonely, sad, angry
All at the same time

Today I'm wearing
My favourite purple shirt
It makes me smile more

Shouting into wind
Took my breath and words away
Exhilarating

Nine and a Half

When I was young
I'd ask my dad
To mark what I'd done
Out of ten

"Nine and a half"
Was always the best
"Always room for improvement"
He'd say

His proudest story
The one with most glory
Was a reference praising
His work as "exemplary"
Why couldn't he say that for me?

"Not good enough"
Is how I took his marks
Mind you, if I'd asked my mum
She'd probably have given me "one"

Between me and you now what I do
Is the best I can do at the time

Rain Pain

why are parents such a pain when it's raining
and I want to go out to play it's good for the
garden they always say when I Grow Up I'll
never put plants ahead of my Children

Secrets

He packed up his secrets
His hopes and his dreams
Neatly
And put them into a pocket
Way down deep in his mind
Where he can always find them
And remind himself
That they are there
Where no one can steal them
And he can never inadvertently
Accidentally
Reveal them

Mum's Cross

Mum is cross today
"Tidy your bedroom" she says
I'll do it later

Rubbish

I feel like rubbish today
Real rubbish,
Not the neat,
Folded-up cardboard kind
That's left out for recycling
More the black mouldy stuff
That grows
After the white furry stuff
On an old Satsuma
That then gets leaky, squoodgy
And smells bad.

The Party – Minnie Mae

Little Minnie Mae
Wandering around
Proclaiming that things are
"'Sgusting"
(She'd heard it from Aunt Mabel
Who sounds rather nasal
When she says the word "disgusting")
This used to be met
With a groan and a frown
But now with gales
Of laughter all round
Which makes her say it
Much more

The Party (Cont'd) – Henri, Flynn and Finn

Henri yearns for paper and pencil
As she's inventing rockets
To go into space
She'll get men, women
And machines
Animals and their needs
Past the moon to Mars
She'd keep them all safe
And feed them
Give them air to breathe
She knows she can get this all done

With Flynn and Finn Finton
(What was their mum thinking)
Having their spooky
Twin thing
Secret language and glances
No chances
That anyone
Will ever break in

The Party (Cont'd) – Barney and Georgia

Barney sits quietly
Fervently hoping
That no-one will ask
Him to play
"He doesn't talk much"
Is what they all say
But that doesn't mean
That his head is empty
It's full of people
And spaces
And places he hasn't
Yet seen

Poor little Georgia
Who is a snorer
Has dropped off
To sleep again
The twins are recording it
Onto their phone
To torment her with
When they get home

The Party (Cont'd) – Leo

Leo hates the attention
Every time someone mentions
His name
He can feel the fear
Tiptoeing up his back
And into his mouth
Making his tongue
Feel so huge
He can barely speak
And wishes the ground would
Swallow him whole
He feels his shoulders, heart
And soul sag
And wishes he was anywhere
Other than here
"Leo the lion"
His mum insists
On calling him
Even though he feels
So much smaller than this
But his stepdad says
"Lying in his bed"
Was the best thing Leo ever did

The Party (Cont'd) – Bem and Benji

Tiny, gurgly, solid Bem
Keeps the adults' attention
As he falls over
Again and again
He loves the applause
As he hauls himself up
Then falls to the floor
Once more
All this is useful
To distract Janie and Dad
As Benji decides to flee
He runs nimbly
Silently up the stairs
To his hideout, his lair
Puts on his headphones
And plays his keyboard
In peace

The Party (Cont'd) – Kamil

Kamil can't bear it
When his stepmum
Treats him a bit
Like a performing seal
She says
"Oh show them Kamil"
And then tells him
To do party tricks
He imagines being
A magician
A painter
A creator of worlds
Especially
How he would love his to be

*What would you write if you chose yourself or a
friend to describe in a verse of this poem?*

Trust Myself

I'm a long way from perfect
I'm sure you can tell
I even get my computer
To check I can spell
Occasionally
(Literally, I once spelt it wrong
In a Fungus the Bogeyman card
I bought for a friend
I was so embarrassed
I went really red
Although nothing was said
I've been really careful
From then on)

But I'm learning to appreciate
Myself for who I am
And not beat myself up
For who I am not

Trust Myself (Cont'd)

I used to try to please
All of the time
'Cos I was always the suspect
In my siblings' crimes
I tried to be invisible
Congenial and perfect

Now I'm older I try to be wiser
I'm more likely to be upset
If I let myself down
Selling myself out
Pretending to be
Someone else

I try not to offend
And still have to blend in
Sometimes of course,
I'm friendly, polite
Considerate and caring
And can often be seen
Wearing a smile

Trust Myself (Cont'd)

I don't tolerate nastiness
Bullying or hate
I try to go my own way
I trust what I think, believe
And hope for

I question myself when conflicts
And dilemmas arise
Which is quite often
When you're an overthinker
Like me
So the myself I think I am
Is constantly changing
Evolving and growing
Who knows who I will become?

Rainbow Wave

When I have worries and cares
That I don't know how to share
These are the things I imagine

I float up to the moon
And sing along with her tune
Or into the ocean deep
Where mermaids sleep

Or fly high up into the sky
With thunder and lightning
And make sky-slashing flashes

Or on the highest most mast
Of the tallest tall ship I stand
With my arms flung out wide
Colours erupt from my sides

Or gaze at the sea and see every wave
Take all of my worries away

Time

Time when I worry
Goes by in a flurry
Of what ifs and maybes

But time at the dentist
Almost feels like it's stopped

When I'm in a hurry
It goes by in the blink
Of a butterfly's wing

But when I'm just waiting
It wears its heaviest boots
And its heaviest heart
And wades though stodgy deep glue

Undies

I really don't know
What the fuss
Is all about
Just 'cos I wear
My underwear
Inside out

Mum takes it as
A personal affront
When I choose to
Wear my undies
Back to front

If she took the time
To think it all through
She'd realise for her
There's less washing to do

One pair of undies
Lasts a whopping
Four days
With so many
Ways to wear them

Worry Hobby

You worry a lot
My mum used to say
Then she would joke
That I could worry about
Not worrying

So I started to say it
And then to believe it
So it became
Almost a hobby for me
Which made it much harder to stop

I wish I could have drawn
Or painted
Written stories
Or poems
Then I could have
Taken the worries
Out for a walk with my pen
And exercise
And exorcise them
At the very same time

Undercover Unicorns

My Granny says that my friends
Are a bunch of lame ducks
She doesn't mean to be rude
She's just a bit old
And says what she's used to saying

My friends are brilliant
I wish adults would grow up
Stop staring at Zac
In his wheelchair
And asking his mum what he wants

Stop stressing when Jimmie
Can't cope with sweetcorn
And peas on his plate
Or when Kemi seems to look
Through you or past you
Rather than at you

Or when Minnie
Is brilliant at maths and physics
But doesn't understand
What being polite is

Undercover Unicorns (Cont'd)

When Micha's legs
Don't work very well
Or when Matthew knows he's under
A goblin's spell

I prefer to think we are
Undercover Unicorns
And when someone
Really sees us
They'll discover
How awesome we are

Zac's unicorn is huge
Fierce and wild
Kemi's changes size
Using all of its senses
Translating the world to her
Minnie thinks unicorns are
Not really needed
She's a superwhizz
At all that matters
And all that is matter
So doesn't understand
The concept of magic

Undercover Unicorns (Cont'd)

Jimmie's a superhero already
Micha likes the idea of a
Jet black unicorn
He can ride at night
And explore the dark
He says
Obviously his can fly
Up through the trees
Into the sky
To see the Earth below
So far up
It's hard to breathe
But from where you can see
Our planet glow

Undercover Unicorns (Cont'd)

Matthew thinks he has magic
Around and within him
So doesn't need one at all

PS my Granny is actually lovely
She says it's her job
And her choice
To love me whatever
Forever and always

Sinking

You know that sinking,
Shrinking, feeling inside
That makes you want to
Run away and hide?
I like to think it means
We're alive
Not just unfeeling machines

When I Get Older

When I get older
I'm going to be the solver
Of the world's problems
I reckon

I'll make sure everyone's fed
And has a warm safe bed
And friends who love them a lot

The seas will be clean
No one will be mean
And we'll eat popcorn day after day

We can work if we want
Or stay home and play
We'll go the moon and Mars and beyond

No one will ask why
We do the things we do
We can adventure and explore
And so much more
'Cos we have the courage to try

Tails

When I feel nervous
I picture people hiding
Tails beneath their clothes

Awesome

Today I am brave
Today I will be awesome
Today I am me

Dragon Wings

As he lies sleeping
He dreams of great dragon wings
Flying wild and free

Be The Bee

Be the bee you want to be
Be the bee you need to be
Not the wasp or the mole
The lion or vole
Or anything else
Others expect you to be

Be the bee you choose to be(e)

Acknowledgements

Everlasting respect, love and thanks to the tiny but mighty Team Elbow. Steve Ward at SW Sounds provided extraordinarily patient professionalism in formatting the book and cover, as well as an occasional gentle edit and inspired design input. Rachel's enthusiasm and support always brings some magic.

Thanks also to Sharon for her comments on an early draft.

Cover Design Charley Elbow and Steve Ward using Gravit Designer, Inkscape and Photoshop.

Thanks to Amazon for setting up a means to make publishing much easier using KDP and Print on Demand.

References

Cheshire Cat, The Hatter and March Hare by Lewis Carroll
The Tortoise and the Hare by Aesop
Hansel and Gretel by The Brothers Grimm
Quidditch from the Harry Potter books by JK Rowling
Little Red Riding Hood by Charles Perrault
Dora the Explorer TV show
Humpty Dumpty Traditional
Little Miss Muffet Traditional

Images

All from Clipart except:

MisKit, Chameleon Cat, Candle, Jupiter, Saturn and Earth – All Pixabay.

Moon (Back Cover) by kind permission of Steve Ward.

37876990R00085

Printed in Poland
by Amazon Fulfillment
Poland Sp. z o.o., Wrocław